us

Tito
the Magician

Guido van Genechten

Clavis

NEW YORK

From the first moment **Tito** saw Manu perform in **Circus Rondo**, he thought Manu was great.

Manu could make things appear out of nowhere.
He sprinkled magic powder, waved his magic
wand over his top hat, said, **"HOCUS POCUS
ABRACADABRA!"** and the most amazing
things came out of the hat. It was unbelievable!

Tito really wanted to know how to do that kind of magic.
At home he sprinkled some magic powder over his little hat,
bravely waved his magic wand, and said,
"HOCUS... POCUS... ABRA CADABRA!"

But nothing happened at all....

No matter how much powder **Tito** used,
and no matter how many times he waved his wand,
his little hat remained empty.

The following morning **Tito** went to Manu's caravan. "Would you teach me how to do magic tricks, Mister Manu?" he asked shyly. "Of course, **Tito**," Manu said, and he immediately got his magic hat and his wand.

"Look carefully," Manu said.
"I'll do the trick in slow motion just for you.
Watch me. First I sprinkle magic powder
on my hat. Then I wave my wand
over it three times.
Like this. And then I say,
**"HOCUS POCUS
ABRACADABRA!"**

Manu pulled a
beautiful white
rabbit out of his
magic hat —
just like that!
Gosh… **Tito** was
astonished. How
could that have
happened?

"Well, **Tito**, did you see what I did?
Can you remember all that?" Manu asked.
"Uh… I… I think so," **Tito** stammered.
"You have to believe that you can do it,"
Manu smiled. "Only then will the magic work."

That evening **Tito** watched
Manu's show again.
This time Manu did a trick with three
little balls and a bunch of flowers.
Suddenly he said, "*Ladies and
gentlemen, please put your hands
together for my new assistant…*"

"...**Tito**!"
The orchestra started
playing, and Manu
gave his cloak, his wand,
and his magic hat to **Tito**.
"Your turn," he whispered.
"It's time for you to do some magic, **Tito**!"
Bravely, **Tito** took his place under the spotlight.

He was nervous, and his hands were trembling. First he sprinkled a little magic powder on the hat. Then he waved his wand three times, exactly the way Manu had shown him.
"HOCUS... POCUS...
ABRA... CADABRA!"
Tito's hand disappeared into the tall hat.
"I know that you can do it, **Tito**," Manu whispered.

And yes, indeed,
all the way down at the bottom
of the hat, **Tito** had conjured
up a real white mouse!

"**Hurray**!" called out Manu.
The audience cheered.
"Hurray for Tito the Magician!"

Tito smiled. He was happy
and proud and excited.
He had made something
appear out of nowhere.
He really could do magic.

First published in Belgium and Holland by Clavis Uitgeverij, Hasselt – Amsterdam, 2005
Copyright © 2005, Clavis Uitgeverij

English translation from the Dutch by Clavis Publishing Inc. New York
Copyright © 2016 for the English language edition: Clavis Publishing Inc. New York

Visit us on the web at www.clavisbooks.com

Tito the Magician written and illustrated by Guido van Genechten
Original title: *Tito tovenaar*
Translated from the Dutch by Clavis Publishing

ISBN 978-1-60537-256-3

This book was printed in April 2016 at Publikum d.o.o., Slavka Rodica 6, Belgrade, Serbia

First Edition
10 9 8 7 6 5 4 3 2 1